Miro and her brothers returned to the grassland, riding on white llamas loaded with riches from the Sun King's bounty. When they reached the hill beside their house, Miro flung the fan into the air where the speckled hawk circled. "I will come soon," she called to her friend. The feathers swirled and danced away toward the *hacha hacha*. Then the three turned down the hill toward their home.

Without a word, he took the flask and strode to where the prince lay.

Two crystal drops splashed into the prince's mouth.

For a moment, he did not move. Then he sat up. "How strong I feel," he said, and drank from the flask.

"*Haylli! Haylli!*" The cry of joy went out.

Miro looked up and saw the golden robes of the Sun King before her.

"Child," the king said, "you must stay forever in my palace and live out your days as one of the daughters of the sun."

Miro was quiet. "Thank you," she said at last, "but here I would be like a yellow monkey on a leash."

The room filled with murmurs, but the Sun King said nothing.

"The greatest reward you could give me," Miro said, "would be to free my brothers and let me go, so that I may travel your great kingdom to see again all the things I have glimpsed on my journey."

The king nodded.

From behind the screen stepped the Sun King. Miro held up the golden flask. "Great King," she said, "I have brought water from the lake at the *pachap cuchun cuchun*."

She followed him through gardens of golden corn and into the palace, down twisting hallways hung with tapestries. "Woven by the daughters of the sun," the servant whispered. Miro stared at the tapestries and at the jungle birds in their cages.

The servant led her to a room where they knelt before a screen. Then he cried out, "O great and very powerful Lord, Child of the Sun, Only Ruler, may all the earth obey you."

As the swirling grains of sand settled, the golden flask
from the palace appeared.

Miro filled the flask with water from the lake. Then she
spread the fan and said, "To Cuzco." She clung to the feathers
until she came to rest on the great smooth Collasuyo Road,
lined with ferny *molle* trees. Sprawled below her, like a lion,
in the bowl of the valley, lay Cuzco.

Around her, she heard the soft slapping of rope sandals,
the whispers of children, and the spitting of llamas with their
loads of dried hot peppers, corn, fruits, and salt. A *chasqui*
runner rushed by with fresh ocean fish for the Sun King's
breakfast. Miro ran behind him, down the paved road, and
into the city. She did not stop running until she reached the
courtyard of the palace. The soldiers lifted their lances, but
when Miro held up the golden flask, a servant ran forward to
lead her in.

Now the air around Miro began to whistle and shriek, and
the sand began to whirl. A winged boa constrictor, red as the
sinking sun, dived out of the sky, screaming, "M-y-y-y-y-y lake!"

Miro raised the feathers high. One tip of a red wing brushed
her ear. Then the snake coiled on the ground and lay still.

Then the surface of the lake bubbled and swirled.

"M-y-y-y-y-y lake," a voice gurgled, and a huge alligator raised its dripping head.

Miro trembled as the beast swam near, but she did not run. She knelt and dipped the fan in the lake. The alligator disappeared in a stream of bubbles.

Before Miro could move, she heard a low moan. "M-y-y-y-y-y lake." Scuttling toward her through the sand was a giant crab as black as the deepest cave.

Her heart began to go *tipuk* but she faced the crab and waved the fan. Instantly, the crab crumpled on the sand.

The air rustled. When Miro opened her eyes, her lap was full of feathers. "We lend these to you," the macaw said. "Do not let go of them."

Miro shaped the feathers into a fan and spread it wide. At once, a wind caught it and lifted Miro out of the tree. Higher than the highest condor she flew, so high that her head ached and her fingers stiffened—but she did not let go of the fan. At last the wind set her down by a lake where the sky came so low it touched the water.

"*Ñaupa pacha,* the One Who Caused Time to Begin, gave the birds a way to help people find the lake at the *pachap cuchun cuchun.*"

"Never!" a honey creeper screeched. "Have you forgotten how the Incas hunt us for our feathers?"

Miro closed her eyes and listened. "This girl knows us," she heard the macaw say. "This is one we will help."

At last, she came to the *hacha hacha* where, as night fell, she climbed a tree. Calling on the moon, wife of the sun, for comfort, she curled up in the branches and slept.

When she woke at dawn, she heard the sound of wings fluttering. "A girl," the birds called to each other. "A girl who will never find what she seeks."

But one scarlet macaw called louder than the rest.

Weeks passed. Each day, Miro would take her favorite llama and climb the terraces to look for her brothers. Then one day, the speckled hawk swooped low, calling out, "News! News!" and Miro heard of her brothers' fate. She packed a bag with corn cakes and potatoes, and when the night was spangled with stars, she slipped out, leading her llama.

All night, they traveled under the constellation of the llama and her lamb. But when the morning star danced before the sun and the *puco puco* bird whistled, Miro heard a puma's cry. Then she turned her llama loose. "Go home," she said as she kissed its nose, "for you will be no puma's dinner."

Miro traveled for days, crossing rope bridges that swayed like giant cobwebs over rivers far below. She climbed high mountains where the air was so thin she could hardly breathe.

The brothers searched the high mountains and the seashore and the deep ravines. They found volcanoes that spewed fire, and people who painted their bodies red with the juice of the *mantur* berry, but they did not find the *pachap cuchun cuchun*. "Surely we have gone farther than anyone," the younger brother finally said. "We should fill a jar with water from any lake. How can it hurt the prince?"

So they brought a jar of water to the Sun King. But as soon as the water was poured into the golden flask, it evaporated. In a rage, the Sun King had the two brothers thrown into a dungeon filled with spiders and scorpions. "Alas for the past," they could be heard crying. "O dungeon, O prison, allow us to go free."

The next day, messengers blew on their conch shells and *chasqui* runners dashed out, the white feathers on their caps streaming behind. "Glory," they cried, "glory for the person who can fill the golden flask with water from the lake at the *pachap cuchun cuchun*."

All over the kingdom, soldiers and knights began the search. Weeks passed, and a few returned with terrible stories of the jungle, the *hacha hacha*, with its jaguars and great boa constrictors. But no one had found the lake.

One day, Miro's eldest brother said to their father, "My brother and I are swift and strong. Perhaps we can find the lake at the *pachap cuchun cuchun*."

"You will be swallowed by the dragon boa constrictor," their father protested. But at last he agreed.

Miro became strong, but in Cuzco the prince grew weak. All the healers with all their arts could not help him. Finally, the Sun King summoned the high priest. "Tell me," he said, "if anything can save my son from this sickness that eats his strength."

The high priest lit a fire. His assistants blew on it through gold and silver tubes, and the high priest spoke into the crackling flames. When he stopped speaking, the fire died away. Lying in the ashes was a golden flask. The high priest said, "Only water from the lake at the *pachap cuchun cuchun*, one of the corners of the earth, drunk from this flask, can save your son."

Then Miro would run outside and, with the llamas, climb high on the terraces where she could call out to the speckled hawk that wheeled overhead. She soon came to understand the speckled hawk's cries and the calls of other birds. "Ho, brothers, sisters!" she would shout, and the birds would swoop low to share their news and tell their legends.

As soon as she was too old to be carried in a cradleboard, she began to run after the guinea pigs that scuttled across the floor. Soon she spent most of her days outside, watching the family llamas and running races with her two older brothers.

"My sons, you are swift runners," their mother would say. "Perhaps, someday you will become *chasqui* runners and carry messages from the wonderful city of Cuzco to the far reaches of the Inca kingdom."

"When will I go to Cuzco?" Miro would ask.

But her mother would say, "Come. Let me show you how to weave."

Ñaupa pacha, once upon a time, in the great city of Cuzco, in the ancient Inca kingdom of Peru, a prince was born to the Sun King. The baby was adorned with red hummingbird feathers and grew up in a palace surrounded by bright jungle birds and yellow monkeys on golden leashes.

Around the same time, a girl named Miro was born in an adobe and stone house by a vast grassland where thousands of llamas grazed.

For my mother, who taught me to love words,
and who has had adventures on five continents
—J. K.

To young Leo, who loves books
—D. F.

AUTHOR'S NOTE

While preparing for a trip to Central America, I came upon an Inca folktale, "The Search for the Magic Lake," told to Genevieve Barlow by descendants of the Inca Indians in Ecuador and re-told by her in *Latin American Folktales* (Rand McNally, 1966). I kept the plot of the story but developed the main character, the girl I named Miro. I also included more about how people in the Inca Empire lived before 1532, the year that Francisco Pizarro and his Spanish soldiers killed the last Inca king.

Text copyright © 1996 by Jane Kurtz
Illustrations copyright © 1996 by David Frampton

All rights reserved. For information about permission to reproduce selections from this book, write to Permissions, Houghton Mifflin Company, 215 Park Avenue South, New York, New York 10003.

For information about this and other Houghton Mifflin trade and reference books and multimedia products, visit The Bookstore at Houghton Mifflin on the World Wide Web at http://www.hmco.com/trade/.

Manufactured in the United States of America

Book design by David Saylor
The text of this book is set in 13-point Minister Bold.
The illustrations are woodcuts reproduced in full color.

HOR 10 9 8 7 6 5 4 3 2 1

LIBRARY OF CONGRESS CATALOGING-IN-PUBLICATION DATA
Kurtz, Jane.
Miro in the kingdom of the sun / by Jane Kurtz ; illustrations by David Frampton.   p.   cm.
Summary: A young Inca girl succeeds where her brothers and others have failed, when her bird friends help her find the special water that will cure the king's son.
ISBN 0-395-69181-8
1. Incas—Folklore.   [1. Incas—Folklore.   2. Folklore—Peru.]
I. Frampton, David, ill.   II. Title.
F3429.3.F6K86   1996
[398.2'089983]—dc20   94-45307   CIP   AC

MIRO IN THE KINGDOM OF THE SUN

BY
JANE
KURTZ

WOODCUTS BY
DAVID
FRAMPTON

HOUGHTON MIFFLIN COMPANY

BOSTON 1996